Disney

Peter Pan

AUTUMN
PUBLISHING

There once was a house in London where the Darling family lived. There were Mr and Mrs Darling and their three children, Wendy, John and Michael.

Watching over the children was Nana, the nursemaid, who also happened to be a dog.

This was the home that Peter Pan often visited.

He chose this house for one very special reason: there were people there who believed in him. Wendy would tell stories of Peter Pan and his adventures in a magical place called Never Land. Peter loved to sit in the shadows and listen.

One night, while the Darling children were sleeping, Peter Pan and his fairy friend, Tinker Bell, slipped into the nursery. Peter had left his shadow behind the last time he visited and had come back to find it.

Suddenly, Wendy woke up. "Peter Pan!" she cried. "I knew you'd come back!" She had been keeping his shadow safe.

Carefully, she sewed Peter's shadow back onto his feet.

Wendy explained to Peter that tonight was her last night in the nursery. "I have to grow up tomorrow," she said.

"I won't have it!" Peter cried. "Come on! We're going to Never Land. You'll never grow up there!"

Wendy woke John and Michael so that they could come too. "But Peter," said Wendy. "How do we get there?"

"Fly, of course!" answered Peter. He sprinkled the children with Tinker Bell's pixie dust and told them to think happy thoughts. Soon they were flying out of the window!

Peter, Tink and the children soared through the skies and finally spotted Never Land.

"There's a pirate ship!" cried Michael.

The captain of the pirate ship was Peter's greatest enemy – Captain Hook!

"Blast that Peter Pan!" said Hook, as he studied a map of Never Land. "If I could only find his hideout, I'd trap him."

Captain Hook got his name because he had a hook where his hand should have been. A hungry crocodile had devoured it long ago, and was still after the rest of him!

Luckily for Hook, there was an alarm clock in the crocodile's belly that went 'tick-tock, tick-tock', so Hook could hear him coming.

Meanwhile, Peter Pan had taken Wendy to see the Mermaid Lagoon. But John and Michael had no interest in mermaids. They wanted an adventure with Peter's friends, the Lost Boys!

"John, you be the leader," cried the Lost Boys. Then, lining up behind him, they marched off into the forest. As they marched along, the Lost Boys and John made a plan. They would be very clever and capture the Natives!

The plan might have worked, too, if the Natives hadn't caught them first! Michael and John were frightened until the Lost Boys explained that it was just a game – the Natives always let them go.

But this time the Chief wouldn't set them free. He thought that they had kidnapped his daughter, Tiger Lily!

Nearby, Peter was showing Wendy the Mermaid Lagoon. Suddenly he spotted Hook and his first mate, Smee, rowing by in a small boat. Tied up in the back was Tiger Lily.

"It looks like they're headed for Skull Rock," Peter said. "Let's see what they're up to."

Sure enough, Hook was holding Tiger Lily prisoner! He had tied her to a rock in the sea and was asking her about Peter Pan's hideout. Hook thought she could tell him where it was.

Peter set off to rescue Tiger Lily before the tide came in.

Peter Pan drew his sword and fought Captain Hook back and forth. Wendy could barely watch and gasped as Hook lunged at Peter.

"I've got you this time, Pan!" cried Captain Hook, forcing Peter near to the edge of a cliff. But Peter danced out of the way, into thin air!

Suddenly, Captain Hook tumbled off the cliff. Smee picked him up in the rowing boat, and the crocodile started to chase them!

While they rowed away, Peter rescued Tiger Lily and flew her back to her father, with Wendy following quickly behind.

The Chief was so pleased to get his daughter back that he gave Peter a headdress and proclaimed him 'Chief Little Flying Eagle'. Wendy, John and Michael watched happily, as their friend received his reward.

But not everyone joined in the celebrations. Back onboard his pirate ship, Captain Hook was hatching an evil plot to get rid of Peter Pan.

Hook had lured jealous Tinker Bell into his lair and promised that he would get rid of Wendy if she would tell him where Peter's hideout was. But as soon as Tink told him, he locked her in a glass lantern!

Meanwhile, at Peter's hideout, Wendy knew that she and her brothers must go home soon. She sang about the wonders of a real mother until even the Lost Boys wanted to go to London! Only Peter wanted to stay.

One by one, the Lost Boys, Wendy, John and Michael left the hideout – only to walk right into the arms of waiting pirates!

Captain Hook and his pirate gang led the prisoners away and tied them to the mast of his ship.

"I have left a little present for Peter," Captain Hook told Smee. "It is due to blast off at six o'clock!"

From her glass prison, Tinker Bell overheard Hook's plan. She was furious! She knocked over the lantern and, with a CRACK, she was free.

Tinker Bell reached Peter's hideout just in time – he was about to open the package! There was no time to explain, so she tried to pull the package away from him.

But it was too late. The box began to smoke. Suddenly – KABOOM!

The explosion was so huge that it rocked Hook's ship from side to side! Captain Hook smiled.

"Join me or walk the plank," Hook shouted to his prisoners.

"Join you? Never!" cried Wendy. She walked to the end of the plank and jumped. But there was no splash...

Peter Pan had flown to save Wendy! He set her down safely, then flew up onto the rigging. Hook scrambled up after him and drew his sword.

As Peter and Hook clashed swords, Wendy, Michael, John and the Lost Boys battled it out with the other pirates.

Suddenly, Captain Hook lost his balance. He fell overboard and into the water, where a familiar crocodile was waiting...

"Hooray for Captain Pan!" cried all the children.

"All right, ya swabs," said Peter. "We're castin' off for London!"

"Michael, John, we're going home!" smiled Wendy.
"Hoist the anchor!" cried Peter. "Tink, let's have some of your pixie dust!"
Tinker Bell flew around the ship, sprinkling her magical dust as she went.
Then, up, up, up went the ship, and as it rose, it began to glow like gold.

Back in London, Mrs Darling found Wendy asleep by the window.

"Oh, Mother, we're back!" cried Wendy. She told her parents all about their wonderful adventure in Never Land.

"I'm going to bed," announced Mr Darling. But as he turned to leave, he noticed, passing in front of the moon, a ship made of clouds...

"You know," said Mr Darling, "I have the strangest feeling I've seen that ship before. A long, long time ago, when I was very young."

And, indeed, he had.